Thomas Ellis Kirby

A grand collection, oriental art objects and curios extraordinary, just received from China and Japan

Antigonos

Thomas Ellis Kirby

A grand collection, oriental art objects and curios extraordinary, just received from China and Japan

Reprint of the original, first published in 1879.

1st Edition 2024 | ISBN: 978-3-38671-487-7

Antigonos Verlag is an imprint of Outlook Verlagsgesellschaft mbH.

Verlag (Publisher): Outlook Verlag GmbH, Zeilweg 44, 60439 Frankfurt, Deutschland, info@outlook-verlag.de
Vertretungsberechtigt (Authorized to represent): E. Roepke, Zeilweg 44, 60439 Frankfurt, Deutschland
Druck (Print): Libri Plureos GmbH, Friedensallee 273, 22763 Hamburg, Deutschland

VANTINE'S
GRAND
Christmas Sale
BIRCH'S
ART GALLERY,
1110 CHESTNUT STREET.
NEW YORK J. J. LITTLE & CO. PRINTERS, 10 TO 20 ASTOR PLACE.

A GRAND COLLECTION

Oriental Art Objects

AND CURIOS

EXTRAORDINARY,

Just received from China and Japan,

PARTICULARLY RICH IN GEMS AND CABINET PIECES,

AND

ARTICLES SUITABLE FOR THE HOLIDAYS.

THE WHOLE TO BE SOLD AT AUCTION, WITHOUT RESERVE,

TOGETHER WITH

A Unique Collection of Kake-Monos,

MOSTLY ANCIENT EXAMPLES,

BY ORDER OF

A. A. VANTINE & CO., IMPORTERS,

On Thursday and Friday Afternoons and Evenings,

Dec. 18 and 19, at 2½ and 7½ o'clock,

AT BIRCH'S ART GALLERY,

No. 1110 CHESTNUT STREET.

ON FREE EXHIBITION DAY AND EVENING.

MR. THOS. E. KIRBY WILL CONDUCT THE SALE.

THOS. BIRCH & SON, AUCTIONEERS.

CONDITIONS OF SALE.

1. The highest Bidder to be the Buyer, and if any dispute arise between two or more Bidders, the Lot so in dispute shall be immediately put up again and resold.

2. The Purchasers to give their names and addresses, and to pay down twenty per cent. on the dollar in part payment, or the whole of the Purchase-money, *if required*, in default of which the Lot or Lots so purchased to be immediately put up again and resold.

3. The Lots to be taken away at the Buyer's Expense and Risk within three days from the conclusion of the Sale, and the remainder of the Purchase-money to be absolutely paid, or otherwise settled for to the satisfaction of the Vendors, on or before delivery: in default of which the Auctioneer will not hold himself responsible if the Lots be lost, stolen, damaged or destroyed, but they will be left at the sole risk of the Purchaser.

4. The Sale of any Painting, Engraving, Print, Furniture, Works of Art, or any other article, is not to be set aside on account of any error in the description. All articles are exposed for Public Exhibition one or more days, and are sold just as they are without recourse.

5. To prevent inaccuracy in delivery no Lot can, on any account, be removed without presentation of bill.

6. Upon failure of complying with the above conditions, the money deposited in part payment shall be forfeited.

THOS. BIRCH & SON.

CATALOGUE.

———

Thursday Afternoon's Sale.

1 Cloisonné enamel Flower Pots, floral design.　　2 pieces
2 Nankin porcelain Teapot, enameled crest decoration.
3 Finely-decorated Hezin porcelain Tea Jar.
4 Set fine Araku Saki Saucers.
5 Chinese crackle ware Bowl, decorated with domestic scenes, etc., in brilliant colors.
6 Bizen Ware, ornamental piece, beggar priest on cow's back.
7 Old Kishiu ware Bottle, basket design, blue and purple glaze. Fine.
8 Handsome cloisonné enamel Plaque, birds and flowers, on imperial blue ground. Diameter 12 inches.
9 Idzmo Vase, very effective design, on crackle ground.
10 Very old Hagi ware Saki Bottle, in form of temple drum. Rare specimen.
11 Celadon Figure, grotesque.
12 Araku Stand, neatly decorated.
13 Rare Vase, cylindrical form, in imitation of bamboo, remarkably raised work, decoration of crabs, grasses, etc. Height 17 inches.
14 Pair brilliantly-decorated fine Arita porcelain Vases, jar shape. Height 18 inches.　　2 pieces
15 Fine old Kutani Plaque, decoration of peacock, pheasant, and peony, in red, gold, yellow, and green. Diameter 12 inches.

16 Cloisonné enamel square Box, fine old Chinese piece, 7x7 inches.

17 Beautifully-decorated Imari porcelain Bowl, richly blended colors, relieved by gold.

18 Small Kishiu Vase, turquoise blue and purple glaze.

19 Pair modern Corean ware Candlesticks, *soufflete* glaze, raised text decoration. Rare. 2 pieces

20 Finely-wrought Japanese bronze Incense Burner, representation of saddle horse.

21 Choice Kiyoto porcelain Rice Jar, hawthorn blossom decoration.

22 Curious Kenzan ware fan-shape Box.

23 Handsomely lacquered and pearl inlaid Dressing Case.

24 Pair fine Japanese cloisonné enamel Tea Jars, floral design on blue ground. 2 pieces

25 Rare Chinese "splash" Vase, bottle shape, *rosedon* glaze. Height 8 inches.

26 Pair crackle ware Vases, enameled decoration of Chinese historical scenes. Height 12 inches. 2 pieces

27 Valuable Chinese Bowl, rich imperial blue glaze, orange peel surface.

28 Corean leaf-shape Trays, crabs, etc., in relief. 2 pieces

29 Fine Idzuma octagonal Tray, enameled decoration of crabs, grasses, etc.

30 Antique Kutani fan-shape Tray, fine old colors.

31 Richly decorated Kaga Teapot.

32 Old Chinese Vase, peculiar effect of splash glaze, turquoise blue over olive green. Height 16 inches.

33 Pair handsome Makudza Vases, cylindrical form, very delicate work of bird-cage, birds, etc. Height 16½ inches.
2 pieces

34 Old Japanese cloisonné enamel deep Plaque, fine in color. Diameter 14 inches.

35 Fine Kiyoto porcelain Bowl, floral decoration.

36 Rare and fine Satsuma Tray, artistic decoration of Japanese mythological scene.

37 Splendid Kaga Bowl, richly decorated, inside and out. Diameter 13 inches.

38 Japanese cloisonné enamel Biberon.

39 Fish-shape Box, white Chinese porcelain, very natural execution.

40 Rare old Bowl, Kirshi-Kawa ware, colored glaze decoration, outside, plain green glaze inside.

41 Chinese porcelain Hanging Vase, basket pattern, rich green glaze, spider's web and spider in gold.

42 Exquisitely decorated Wakayama ware Jar, ornamentation in gold and colors on beautiful yellow ground. Height 14 inches.

43 Pair handsomely painted Hezin porcelain Vases, decorated with figures of dog Foo, willow tree, lotus flowers, etc. Height 18 inches.   2 pieces

44 ELEGANT ARITA PORCELAIN PLAQUE, richly ornamented with gold and silver on black lacquer ground. Diameter 25 inches.

45 Handsomely enameled Nankin porcelain large Bowl, green glaze within.

46 Kenzan ware Sectional Box, 2 compartments, decorated with red, green, gray, etc., on creamy ground.

47 Rare Chinese Vase, enameled decoration of vines, etc., on dull chocolate glaze. Height 10 inches.

48 Pair Owari porcelain Vases, choice porcelain and fine blue decoration. Height 10 inches.   2 pieces

49 ELEGANT UMBRELLA STAND, finest Hezin porcelain, exquisitely decorated with birds, butterflies, and flowers, on dull black ground, richly lacquered panels. Height and diameter 27x8 inches.

50 Pair large Vases, finest Arita porcelain, brilliantly decorated, character medallions. Height 30 inches.   2 pieces

51 Yeiraku Fire Bowl, very artistic decoration of crysanthemums, on bright yellow.

52 Handsome Plaque, Kioyaki ware, very fine decoration of storks, hawthorn, etc. ; very decorative. Diameter 20 inches.

53 Awata ware Tea Jar, handsomely decorated with flowers, etc.

54 Fine *Bleu de Nankin* Rice Bowl and Cover.

55 Valuable Chinese " Splash " Vase, triple gourd shape, rich *rosedon* glaze, shading into purple. Height 18 inches.

56 Pair handsome Satsuma Vases, made by the celebrated Makudza, raised decoration of old bamboo hat, dragon fly, locust, and other insects ; very naturally executed. Height 16 inches.   2 pieces

57 Handsome Owari porcelain Tête-à-tête Set, exquisitely decorated in blue and gold.

58 Finely-carved Kiyaki Wood Tray, lotus leaf form.

59 Rich crimson and gold decorated Kaga Bowl.

60 Old Chinese cloisonné enamel Vase, trumpet shape, well preserved specimen. Height 12 inches.

61 Antique Fire Pot, wood carving, representation of wooden bell which was used in Buddhist temples.

62 Elegant mulberry wood Cabinet, with 5 drawers and enclosure, front surface ornamented with 38 fine specimens of intricate metal work, 16x18x9 inches.

63 Very old Kutani Plaque, decoration of landscape in various colors. Diameter 13 inches.

64 ELEGANT VASE, pure white Kenzan ware, raised decoration of Shikunshi, top and lower part decorated in crimson and gold. Height 12 inches.

65 Pair handsome Vases, Japanese cloisonné on porcelain, flowers, leaves, etc., in fan-shaped medallion, chickens in relief at base. Height 11 inches.   2 pieces

66 Set elegant after-dinner Coffee Cups and Saucers, finest porcelain and richest Chinese decoration ; sold with handsome case made of Japanese fabrics, as   8 pieces

67 Arita porcelain Bowl, finely decorated.

68 Awata ware Flower Baskets.   2 pieces

69 ELEGANT NAGASAKI VASE, exquisite decoration of bamboo branches, etc., on imperial yellow glaze. Height 7 inches.

70 Pair skillfully wrought silver bronze small Vases, inlaid with precious metals. Height 10 inches.   2 pieces

71 Rare Plaque, "Kioyaki," peculiar decoration of moon and waves of the sea carved out before the glaze was spread over. Diameter 14 inches.

72 Exquisitely decorated Awata ware Bowl, lotus form.

73 Pair Owari porcelain Saki Bottles, blue decoration.

74 Cochin China Tray, incised decoration, green glaze, rare specimen.

75 EXCEEDINGLY FINE SATSUMA VASE, gourd shaped, remarkably fine decoration of bold figures, etc. Height 12 inches.

76 Pair unusual Vases, vine decoration in relief, open work bowls, brown glaze. Height 13 inches.   2 pieces

77 Handsome silver bronze Plaque, artistically inlaid with gold and silver. Diameter 12 inches.

78 Large oblong Plaque, blue Ninshei ware, rare and old piece. 14x20 inches.

79 Elegant lacquered Cabinet, ornamented with pure gold.

80 Pair handsome Hezin porcelain Vases, decorated in very brilliant colors. Height 15 inches.   2 pieces

81 Fine Satsuma Plaque, embossed and finely painted decoration, damio figure.

82 Nankin porcelain small Plates, neatly decorated.   12 pieces

83 Modern Kishin ware Saki Bottle, "splash" glaze, blue and purple.

84 Finely enameled Nankin jewel Trays.   2 pieces

85 Handsome Awata ware Tête-à-Tête Set, enameled decoration, sold with lacquered Tray.

86 Artistically wrought Gorosa bronze Mantel Set, comprising elegant centre piece and two vases. 3 pieces

87 Choice Hezin porcelain Bowl, handsomely decorated.

88 Pair Nankin small cylinder Vases, character decoration on unusual pink glaze. 2 pieces

89 Owari porcelain Tea Jars, fine blue decoration, reticulated panels. 2 pieces

90 Rare and valuable *rosedon* Plaque, orange peel surface, exceedingly fine in color.

91 Small cloisonné enamel Vase, unusual shape, fine work on Kiyoto ware.

92 Pair choice Celadon Vases, lotus form. Height 9 inches. 2 pieces

93 SUPERB CLOISONNÉ ENAMEL PLAQUE, beautiful design of flying birds, morning-glory vines, etc., on peacock blue ground, rich combination of colors in border. Diameter 15 inches. Finest quality of work.

94 —— Another, smaller, different design.

95 Valuable old Satsuma Bowl, exquisitely decorated, mounted in Japanese fabric case.

96 SPLENDID NAGASAKI VASE, jar shape, beautifully decorated with flying storks, lotus plants, etc., lavender glaze, gold clouding. Height 10 inches.

97 PAIR ELEGANT CHINESE CLOISONNE ENAMEL VASES, biberon form, rich floral design on blue ground. Height 13 inches. 2 pieces

98 Richly decorated Imari porcelain Bowl, high form.

99 HIGHLY VALUABLE OLD SATSUMA KORA (Incense Burner), globular form, on tripod support, artistically painted and embossed decoration of figures, Buddhist priest, flowers, etc., figure of dog Foo surmounting cover. Height and diameter 20x16 inches. Ancient and exceedingly fine specimen of this rare ware.

100 Pair elegantly carved Gorosa bronze Vases, cylindrical form, on movable bases, stork, flying birds, etc., in bold relief. Height 20 inches. 2 pieces

Unique Cabinet Specimens.

GEMS IN METAL WORK, IVORY, LACQUER, JADE, ETC.

101 Small Corean Trays, raised crabs. 2 pieces
102 Tortoise-shell small round Tray, exquisite gold lacquer ornamentation.

103 Wakiyama small Tray, incised decoration, mustard yellow glaze.

104 Carved wood Netsuke Mask.

105 Corean small pitcher, splash glaze.

106 Old earthen Box, imitation of wood.

107 Exquisitely decorated Nagasaki small Vase, rich green glaze.

108 Gorosa bronze small leaf-shaped Tray, finely wrought.

109 Fine Satsuma Bowl, raised work decoration of crabs.

110 Superb gold lacquer Saki Bottle, engraved ornamentation of Tycoon's crest.

111 Exquisitely carved ivory Card-case.

112 Fine green jade-stone Cup.

113 Handsome Ohta ware Bowl, artistically decorated in enamel and raised work.

114 Small ivory tusk Vase, gold lacquer ornamentation.

115 Pair rare and fine cloisonné enamel small Vases, design of cherry tree in blossom, crysanthemums, etc., on translucent enamel, black ground border. 2 pieces

116 Ancient wrought-iron Box, skillfully inlaid with gold and silver, $1\frac{1}{2}$x3x$4\frac{1}{2}$ inches. Rare and fine specimen.

117 Exquisitely decorated Ohta ware Bowl, open-work border, has been broken, and neatly repaired.

118 Handsome lacquered Card-case, fruit in relief, on b'ack ground, monkeys and gold inlaying on reverse side. Remarkably fine.

119 Valuable Jade-stone Vase, bottle shape, finely carved. Height, with teak-wood stand, 6 inches.

120 Rare Araku Tea Jar, beautifully lacquered ornamentation on jet black glaze.

121 Pair very fine Kaga porcelain small Vases exquisitely decorated. 2 pieces

122 Superb carved ivory small Vase, cylindrical form, fine work, by Chinese artist.

123 Very rare Satsuma Saki Bottle, wonderfully modeled ornamentation in raised work of turtle, crab, frog, etc.

124 Splendid beaten silver Tray, lotus leaf form, exceedingly fine workmanship and rare color.

125 Choice Piece of Color, small porcelain Vase, pink glaze ornamentation in white, has teak-wood stand.

126 Beautiful Exhibition Plaque, exquisitely decorated in alternate stripes, partial lavender glaze, sold with case.

127 Fine specimen of cloisonne enamel, vine and leaves on solid silver base, translucent enamel.

128 —— Another specimen, smaller, fan shape.

129 Superb Kiyoto porcelain Cup, decorated in pure gold.

130 Fine white jade stone Bowl.

131 Beautiful lacquered egg shape Tray, decoration of insects.

132 Handsome cloisonne enamel bronze Tea Jar, design of morn-
ing-glories and butterflies on imperial blue ground.

133 Exceedingly fine Satsuma Bowl, raised work decoration of
octopus, carp fish, etc.

134 Small iron Vase, beautifully inlaid with gold and silver, very
artistic work.   Height 7 inches.

135 Choice black and gold lacquer Perfume Box, metal lined.

136 Extremely fine Ivory Carving, Buddhist priest and tiger, old
and artistically executed.

137 Japanese leather Cigar Case, lacquered ornamentation.

138 UNIQUE METAL VASE, showing the different processes of
cloisonne enamel.   Height 5 inches.   Valuable specimen.

139 Choice Nagasaki porcelain Saki Bottle, decoration of dragon,
clouds, etc.

140 MOST VALUABLE COREAN SPECIMEN, antique Teapot,
with wonderful raised work ornamentation of frogs at com-
bat, etc., one of the finest specimens of this work in the sale

141 Finely-wrought silver and iron Medicine Box, lozenge shape,
inlaid with bronze and precious metals.

142 Set very fine egg-shell porcelain Saki Saucers, decorated with
figures of the seven household gods.   7 pieces

143 SUPERB LACQUERED TRAY, round form, center most exquisitely ornamented with pure gold and inlaid with pearl,
border in imitation of steel, with decoration of flying storks
and pine trees in black.   Diameter 9 inches.

---

144 Beautifully embroidered drab satin Table Cover. 54x54 inches.

145 Handsome crape Table Cover, pearl color, with beautifully-
illuminated border, 4½x4½ feet.

146 Fine square Embroidery, birds and flowers on b'ack satin.

147 —— Another, larger and finer, flowers in fan medallions,
worked in brilliant silks and gold bullion, on rich plum
color silk.

148 Elegant crape screen Center or Hanging, flowers, fruit, etc.;
painted and embroidered in very rich colors.

149 —— Another, equally as fine, different co'or and design.

150 VERY ELEGANT IMARI PORCELAIN INCENSE BUR-
NER, globular form on tripod, bowl and cover reticulated
and ornamented in relief with birds and flowers, dragon
handles and in relief on cover, all decorated in richly
blended colors relieved by gold.   Height and diameter
18x15 inches.

151 Finely carved teak-wood Stand, marble top, inlaid.

152 PAIR MAGNIFICENT CLOISONNE ENAMEL LARGE
 VASES, exceedingly fine in design and color, interesting
 form, and highest class of Chinese workmanship on bronze.
 Height 24 inches. 2 pieces

152a Handsomely painted Screen, high form, 4 folds, black ground.

152b —— Another, 2 folds, white ground.

Thursday Evening's Sale.

153 Kaga Saki Cups, finely decorated. 2 pieces

154 Cloisonne enamel porcelain Toilet Boxes. 2 pieces

155 Neat'y decorated Awata Cigar Trays. 2 pieces

156 Yakonin porcelain Cigar Ash Cups. 2 pieces

157 Antique Hibiki Bowl, gray g'aze, blue decoration. Rare.

158 Crackle ware fine Bowl, enamel decoration.

159 Finely enameled Nankin porcelain Jewel Stands. 2 pieces

160 Choice Kiyoto porcelain Bowl, handsomely decorated.

161 Rare and fine Chinese antique crackle ware small Vase, bottle-
 shape, character decoration.

162 Pair neatly enameled Awata-ware small Vases, cylindrical
 shape. 2 pieces

163 Exquisitely decorated Kiyoto porcelain basket-shape Trays.
 2 pieces

164 Exceedingly fine specimen of cloisonne enamel small Perfume
 Jar, emb'ematical design on imperial blue ground, sold
 with Japanese fabric case.

165 Rare Chinese bottle-shape Vase, rich olive-brown "splash"
 glaze.

166 Carved lacquer Tray, inlaid with pearl.

167 Curious hanging Vase, representation of cucumber.

168 Ancient Japanese cloisonne enamel Plaque, fine in color.
 Diameter 13 inches.

169 Very fine Kaga Saki Bottle, exquisitely decorated in crimson
 and gold.

170 Pair handsome cloisonné enamel porcelain Tea Jars. 2 pieces

171 Corean ware Trays, lotus leaf form, fishes in relief, two colors
 of glaze. 2 pieces

172 Rare and fine Nagasaki Vase, canteen shape, enameled decoration of dragons, clouds, etc.

173 Pair fine modern Satsuma Vases, neat decoration of crysanthemum flowers. Height 10 inches. 2 pieces

174 Richly decorated Kaga Bowl.

175 Antique Nankin porcelain Plate, basket-work border, choice
blue decoration.

176 VALUABLE COREAN TRAY, leaf shape on feet, exceedingly fine
raised work, ornamentation of shells, pickle, etc. Rare.

177 Ancient Chinese cloisonné enamel Bowl, slightly defective.

178 Handsome Banko Plaque, enameled decoration of crayfish,
artistically modeled and very life-like. Diameter 15 inches.

179 Old Yatzshin ware Vase, curiously glazed. Height 14 inches.
Very rare specimen.

180 Pair beautifully decorated Kiyoto porce'ain Vases, enameled
decoration of storks flying, birds, and floweis, gold clouding, ring handles. Height 14 inches.

181 Fine Bowl, old Chinese "Green Family," dragon and emble-
matic ball outside, "Howo" bird inside. Diameter 9
inches.

182 Splendid Japanese cloisonné enamel Plaque, design of dragon-
fly, blossoms, etc., on blue ground. Diameter 15 inches.

183 —— Another, smaller, design of flowers, flying birds, etc., on
dark-blue ground.

184 Handsomely decorated Arita porcelain sweetmeat Jar.

185 Choice blue decorated Tête-à-Tête Set, with lacquered Tray.

186 Very old and finely decorated large Satsuma Bowl, va'uable
specimen.

187 Richly ornamen'ed Hezin porcelain umbrella Vase, elegant
lacquered decoration. Height 24 inches.

188 Pair elegant Hezin porcelain Vases, artistica'ly decorated in
brilliant colors. Height 20 inches. 2 pieces

189 Curious po tery Incense Burner, representing gluttonous bear.

190 Brilliantly decorated Arita porcelain large Plaque, Japanese
hunting scene. Diameter 16 inches.

191 Rare Banko-Yaki Basket, form of lotus leaf, stems forming
handle, bud in relief, natural color glaze.

192 SPLENDID SATSUMA INCENSE BURNER, decoration of the most
exquisite character, beautiful form and exceedingly fine
creamy clay, figure of dog Foo on cover. Height and diameter 13x10 inches.

193 PAIR SUPERB JAPANESE CLOISONNE ENAMEL
VASES, beautiful design of birds, flowers, bamboo tree,
etc., on peacock blue ground, rich'y combined borders top
and bottom, work of a thoroughly ar istic order. Height
12 inches.

194 Old Nankin large Bowl, decoration of Chinese poetess, birds, flowers, etc.

195 Fine Seto porcelain Jar and Cover, rich blue decoration beneath glaze.

196 Ohta-ware Figures, Buddhist priests.   2 pieces

197 Curious wrought Bronze Candlestick. "The long armed man."

198 Beautifully decorated Imari porcelain Sweetmeat Box, square form on butterfly feet.

199 Handsome Cabinet, finely inlaid with various woods, has three shelves, 4 drawers and enclosures, 13x24x10 inches.

200 Pair large Vases, finest Hezin porcelain, handsomely decorated with birds, flowers, etc., carefully painted in bright colors. Height 30 inches.   2 pieces

201 Handsome Awata ware after dinner Cups and Saucers, enameled decoration, butterfly handles.   12 pieces

202 Finest quality black lacquer oblong Tray with rim and handle, exquisite gold ornamentation.

203 Finely painted Arita porcelain irregular shaped Plaque.

204 Superbly decorated Kiyota porcelain Goblet-shaped Vase.

205 Pair wonderfully wrought Saymin bronze Vases, Japanese rain dragon in relief. Height 12 inches.   2 pieces

206 Beautiful lacquered panel, Basket full of favorite Japanese fruits, very closely represented, butterflies in mother of pearl, example of the famous lacquer artist Yagami Lozan, 12x22 inches.

207 Superb specimen Plate, choicest porcelain, exquisite decoration of flowers and birds, an artistic production. Sold with case.

208 Very fine Nagasaki porcelain Tête-à-Tête Set, handsomely decorated with bamboo branches in black and gold. Sold with carved wood Tray.

209 Rare and valuable Chinese Tea Jar, rich *rosedon* " splash " glaze.

210 Finely wrought Japanese bronze Incense Burner, dragon supporting jar.

211 Beautiful Owari porcelain Teapot, high form, decorated in rich blue color, and ornamented with black and gold lacquer medallions.

212 Splendid Vase, rich brown metallic luster, choicest porcelain. Height 12 inches. Rare and exceedingly fine.

213. Pair handsome Makudza Vases, beautifully wrought decoration of bird on Zakuro tree. Very delicate workmanship. Height 13 inches.   2 pieces

214 ELEGANT CLOISONNE LARGE PLAQUE, design of birds, morning glory, vines, etc., on turquoise blue, beautiful combination of colors in border. Diameter 18 inches.

215 Fine Nankin porcelain Bowl and Cover, willow tree and character decoration.

216 SPLENDID LITTLE VASE, fine old Satsuma ware, exceedingly fine ornamentation of insects, in raised work. Height 8 inches.

217 Pair Chinese antique crackle ware small Vases, decorated with domestic scenes, etc. 2 pieces

218 Handsomely-decorated Hezin porcelain hexagonal Tray.

219 Choice blue decorated Owari porcelain Fire Bowl.

220 MARVELOUSLY-WROUGHT BRONZE VASE, low square form, bold figure of rain dragon in relief, example of the famous Saymin, 5½x8 inches; exceedingly valuable specimen.

221 Handsome carved wood sectional Chow-Chow Box, jar shape, 5 compartments, black and gold lacquer ornamentation.

222 Ancient Araku Fire Bowl, rich enameled decoration.

223 Rare Chinese imperial yellow Plate, incised decoration of dragon.

224 Superb Nagasaki porcelain Sweetmeat Jar, beautiful enameled decoration of blossoms, etc.

225 RARE AND CURIOUS SPLASH VASE, peculiar effect of turquoise glaze. Height 15 inches.

226 Pair elegantly-decorated Arita porcelain Vases, ruffle tops. Height 16 inches.

227 Fine Seto porcelain Plaque, decoration beneath glaze, in choice blue. Diameter 14 inches.

228 Exquisitely decorated Kiyoto porcelain Cup and Cover.

229 Very fine antique Imari Perfume Jar, decorated with choice colors.

230 Handsomely enameled Banko Vase, brown glaze, storks, lotus flowers in relief.

231 Pair choice blue decorated Owari porcelain Vases. Height 10 inches. 2 pieces

232 Splendid Bowl, cloisonné art on porcelain, rich in design and rare colors, blue and gold decoration inside. Diameter 6 inches.

233 Kiyoto ware Tete-a-tete Set, neatly decorated, sold with black and gold lacquer Tray.

234 Handsome carved lacquer Tray, very fine specimen; should be closely examined.

235 Beautiful Mekawatch Bowl and Plate, crysanthemum form, decoration of a most exquisite character.

236 ARTISTICALLY DECORATED SATSUMA INCENSE BURNER, in form
of temple drum, dragons in relief on sides, figure of chicken
cock surmounting cover.   6x12 inches.

237 Pair finely wrought Chinese bronze Vases, birds, branches, and
blossoms in relief.   Height 13 inches.   2 pieces

238 Fine cloisonné enamel porcelain Cups.   2 pieces

239 Rare celadon Plate, decorated with bold figures, willow tree,
etc.

240 Finely painted Daimio Folding Screen, low form, used at the
festival of dolls, Japan.

241 ELEGANT KAGA PUNCH BOWL, artistically decorated with very
brilliant colors relieved by pure gold.   Diameter 18 inches.

242 Valuable old Kishiu Vase, turquoise blue glaze, incised decoration.   Height 12 inches.

243 Pair handsomely decorated Yeddo Vases, elephant head
handles.   Height 14 inches.   2 pieces

244 Magnificent Daimio Sword, superior blade, fine black lacquer
scabbard, exquisitely wrought gold and silver mountings.

245 —— Another, larger.

246 —— Another, sharkskin scabbard.

247 Handsome black and gold lacquer Sword Rack, for three
swords.

Gems and Unique Cabinet Speci-
mens.

248 Ancient Japanese pottery Teapot in imitation of wood.

249 Red and gold lacquer Saki Saucer.

250 Jade-stone cylinder Vase.

251. Exquisitely lacquered round Tray.

252 Choice cloisonne enamel small Vase, floral design on rare
imperial yellow ground.

253 Pair antique crackle-ware small Vases, brown glaze, character
decoration.   2 pieces

254 Rare Imakura Box and Cover, neatly decorated.

255 Finely carved jade-stone Ring, rare in color.

256 Fine old Satsuma Bowl, decorated with boldly drawn figure,
etc.

257 Exquisitely decorated Kiyoto porcelain Flower Pail, an exceedingly fine specimen of decorated art.

258 HANDSOME IVORY VASE, artistically carved by Chinese artist.

259 Finely decorated Ohta ware Bowl.

260 Very fine Satsuma small Incense Burner, unusually fine decoration of goddess of heaven, dragon, etc.

261 Small Japanese cloisonné enamel Vase, bottle shape, fine work on bronze.

262 RARE AND VALUABLE COREAN JAR AND COVER, remarkable raised-work ornamentation of fishes, etc.

263 Handsome cloisonné Tea Jar, design of storks and pine tree on imperial blue ground.

264 Choice Nagasaki Vase, cylindrical form, enameled decoration of bamboo branch, etc., on dull black glaze.

265 ELEGANT OHTA-WARE PLAQUE, most exquisitely decorated with gold and delicate colors, example of the famous Tai-Zau. Diameter 14 inches. Valuable specimen, should be carefully examined.

Elegant Embroideries.

266 Rich black satin Table Cover, beautifully embroidered with storks, pheasants, flowers, and blossoms in gold bullion and brilliant silks. 6x6 feet.

267 Handsome blue crape Table Cover, beautiful illuminated border. 52x52 inches.

268 Profusely embroidered daimio Robe, fine work on green crape.

269 Handsome crape Hanging or Screen, center beautifully embroidered, painted flowers. 27x36 inches.

270 Japanese paper Table Cover, painted border.

271 —— Another.

272 ELABORATE PALACE HANGING, wonderful specimen of needlework, Buddhist subject embroidered in gold bullion and silk. 55x78 inches.

273 —— Another.

---

274 Japanese warrior's Lance, lacquered pole and bronze mountings.

275 —— Another.

276 Spear carried by daimio attendants.

277 —— Another.

278 Set handsomely decorated Chinese Teapoy Tables, black and gold. 4 pieces

279 —— Another set, different. 4 pieces

280 —— Another set, red. 4 pieces

281 Richly painted Screen, high form, 3 folds, white ground.

282 —— Another. 2 folds, white linen ground.

283 LARGE AND VALUABLE HIOGO CRACKLE VASE, celadon glaze, white medallions. Height and diameter 18x28 inches.

284 Pair handsome Arita porcelain large Vases, handsomely painted and lacquered panels.   Height 33 inches.   2 pieces

Kake-Monos

(Hanging Scrolls),

Mostly Ancient Examples, Painted on Silk, and Richly Mounted.

285 Kake-mono, landscape.

286 —— Another, very fine India-ink sketch, "rain dragon."

287 —— Another, Daimio lady and servant.

288 —— Another, Daimio figure, landscape view, etc., in colors.

289 —— Another, mountain scenery.

290 —— Another, stork, grasses, etc.

291 —— Another, exceedingly fine group of chickens.

292 —— Another, highly illuminated, Buddhist subject.

293 —— Another, figure of Japanese poet.

294 —— Another, ink sketch of horse.

295 —— Another, miniature painting, death of Buddha.

296 —— Another, stork on pine-tree branch, exceedingly fine India-ink sketch.

297 —— Another, ink sketch, Japanese rice merchant.

298 Another, storks, water lilies, etc.

299 Another, very large, containing over 1,000 figures of Buddha.

300 Another, larger and finer, lamentation of Japan over the death of Buddha.

———— - - —

Friday Afternoon's Sale.

301 Awata ware Toilet Boxes.   2 pieces

302 Banko-Yaki Teapots, enameled decoration.   2 pieces

303 Exquisitely decorated Kaga Saki Goblets.   2 pieces

304 Neatly decorated Nankin porcelain small plates.   12 pieces

305 Black and gold lacquer small Flower Vase.

306 Fine blue decorated Nankin porcelain Mugs.   2 pieces

307 Ohta Bowl, finely decorated.

308 Handsome Corean Incense Burner, *soufflée* glaze, incised decoration.

309 Pair "Bleu de Nankin" Vases, antique forms.   Height 8 inches.   2 pieces

310 Richly decorated Kaga Bowl.

311 Brilliantly painted Hezin porcelain Plaque. Diameter 14 inches.

312 Exquisitely decorated Kiyoto porcelain small Vase, on bamboo feet.

313 Pair Chinese antique crackle small Vases, mustard brown glaze, imitation bronze ornamentation.   2 pieces

314 Beautifully decorated Kiyoto porcelain Tête-à-Tête Set, sold with lacquered tray.

315 Pair fine cloisonné enamel small Flower Pots.

316 Chinese porcelain small cylinder Vases, character and text decoration.   2 pieces

317 Silver bronze Plate, inlaid with gold and silver.

318 Carved wood Saki Bottle, gourd shape, black and gold lacquer ornamentation.

319 Rare Imakura Vase, ovoid form on tripod, curious effect of splash glaze.   Height 11 inches.

320 Pair Chinese crackle ware Vases, white glaze decorated with Chinese domestic scenes in brilliant colors.   Height 12 inches.   2 pieces

321 Handsome Nagasaki oblong Plaque, rich brown and gold lacquer ornamentation, 15x17 inches.

322 Pair fine Japanese cloisonné enamel porcelain tea Jars, floral design on blue ground.   2 pieces

323 Fine Pekin enamel Confection Service and Table Center combined.   7 pieces

324 Nice little splash Vase, bottle shaped, rich color of glaze.

325 Handsomely decorated Hezin porcelain after-dinner Coffee Cups and Saucers.   12 pieces

326 Finest quality black and gold lacquer oblong Tray, with rim.

327 Exquisitely decorated Kiyoto porcelain tea or dessert Plates, fan pattern center.   12 pieces

328 Splendid Imari porcelain Bowl, low form, exceedingly fine decoration.

329 Fine Owari porcelain Bottle, choicest blue color, decoration beneath glaze.

2

330 Handsome cloisonné enamel Plaque, finest Japanese workmanship on bronze, rich design of flowers, butterfly, etc., on
blue ground.   Diameter 15 inches.

331 —— Another, small fan-shape medallions.

332 Valuable antique bronze Vase, wonderfully wrought dragon
handles, peculiar effect of lacquer intermingled with the
bronze while molten.   Height 8 inches, rare and exceedingly
fine specimen.

333 PAIR VERY ELEGANT NAGASAKI VASES, most exquisite and artistic decoration of flying birds, eagle, landscape scenery, etc., gold clouding and bands, ring handles.
Height 13 inches, exceedingly fine, from the Nagasaki exhibition.

334 Ancient Corean Kora, carved ivory figure and leaves in relief on
cover.

335 Kutani Bowl and Cover, finely decorated inside and out.

336 Tea Jar, ancient Nebshima porcelain, decorated with finely
painted figures of Buddhist priests, deity, etc., on red
glaze, rare.

337 PAIR UNUSUAL SATSUMA BEAKERS, exquisite gold decoration
and leaves in raised work.   Height 7 inches.   2 pieces

338 SET RICHLY DECORATED CUPS AND SAUCERS IN HANDSOME CASE,
finest porcelain and best Chinese decoration sold as

7 pieces

339 Elegant dessert Plates, decorated to match, finest Berlin china,
open work borders.   12 pieces

340 Handsome Nankin porcelain punch Bowl, richest Chinese
decoration, has carved teakwood stand.

341 Ancient Japanese cloisonne enamel cylindrical Vase on lacquered stand, fine in color.

342 VERY ELEGANT SILVER BRONZE MANTEL SET, skillfully mani-
pulated and inlaid with precious metals, comprises center
piece and two vases, sold as   3 pieces

343 BEAUTIFULLY DECORATED EXHIBITION PLAQUE, painting of fish,
bird, flowers, etc., artistically executed.   Diameter 8 inches.
Sold with case.

344 SUPERB KAGA FLOWER VASE, profuse decoration of flying
storks, beautifully painted in rich colors relieved by gold.
Height and diameter, 7x8 inches. .

345 PAIR SPLENDID CLOISONNE ENAMEL VASES, unusual form and
very fine in colors and design.   Height 15 inches. 2 pieces

346 MOST VALUABLE SATSUMA PLAQUE, DECORATED
IN A MASTERLY MANNER WITH BUST OF BUD-
DHIST PRIEST, AND FIGURE OF DEITY, EXE-
CUTED IN RICH COLORS OF ENAMEL AND GOLD
EMBOSSED WORK.   DIAMETER 20 INCHES.   AN
OLD AND HIGHLY VALUABLE SPECIMEN.

Extraordinary Cabinet Specimens,

INCLUDING MANY OBJECTS PROCURED AT THE NAGASAKI EXHIBITION.

347 Exquisite lacquer Saki Saucer.

348 Rare Imakura Bowl, engraved and enameled decoration.

349 Valuable small Chinese Jar, lemon color glaze.

350 Old Satsuma Medicine Box, mice and carrot in relief on cover. Rare and fine.

351 Green jade Cup, finely carved and polished.

352 Japanese bronze Scarf Pin, exquisitely wrought and inlaid with gold and silver.

353 —— Another.

354 Pure gold lacquer miniature Perfume Box.

355 Unusually fine old Japanese cloisonne enamel Plate.

356 Ancient wrought Iron Box, beautifully inlaid with gold and silver. 2x3x5 inches.

357 Small Nagasaki jar-shape Vase, bamboo branch decoration on canary color glaze, has teak-wood stand.

358 Fine Kiyoto porcelain goblet-shape Vase, lavender color glaze, with delicate pink clouding, floral and text decoration in white.

359 Superb lacquered Card Case, choice specimen.

360 Small ivory tusk Vase, exceedingly fine gold lacquered ornamentation.

361 Beautiful "Imari white" porcelain Perfume Jar, enameled decoration of flying birds.

362 Very fine and ancient Chinese cloisonné Teapot, quaint shape and well preserved specimen.

363 Valuable carved jade Vase, bottle shape, fine green color. Height 5 inches.

364 Superb gold decorated Kiyoto porcelain Cup, mounted in Japanese fabric case.

365 Rare antique Kiyoto Bowl, raised-work decoration of flying bats, etc., gold moon, fine specimen, slightly defective, has silk case.

366 Artistically carved ivory Group, Japanese historical subject.

367 RARE SPECIMEN OF COLOR, small crackle Vase, with beautiful pink glaze.

368 Small cloisonné enamel Fire Bowl, emblematical design on black ground, brass mountings, fine specimen.

369 Pair choice modern Satsuma small Vases, rich gold embossed decoration. Height 6 inches. 2 pieces

370 SUPERB PURE GOLD LACQUER DAIMIO PERFUME Box, lozenge shape. 2x3x5 inches. A valuable specimen of old lacquer, showing most delicate workmanship.

371 Neatly lacquered small Trays. 2 pieces

372 SPLENDID CLOISONNÉ ENAMEL BOWL AND COVER, gold lined and bronze base in form of lotus leaf, workmanship of the highest order, and beautifully combined colors. Height and diameter 7x4½ inches.

373 Artistically decorated Satsuma Bowl, figure of god of plenty, Japanese children, etc., inside.

374 SPLENDID BIT OF COLOR, small Perfume Jar, beautiful shade of *rosedon* glaze, exceedingly rare.

375 Handsome lacquer Box, round flat form, raised ornamentation of fruits, etc., inside and out, gold inlaid handle and cover. Diameter 8 inches. Old and rare.

376 Valuable Corean Bowl, remarkable raised work, decoration of frogs, crab, etc.

377 Exquisitely carved ivory Vase, cylindrical form, fine work by Chinese artist.

378 Neatly lacquered Flower Pail.

379 UNUSUAL SPECIMEN OF COLOR, small ovoid form Vase, imperial yellow crackle glaze. Height 6 inches.

380 Very fine "grains of rice" Bowl, Cover and Stand, choice blue decoration, unusual specimen, and valuable.

381 VALUABLE SATSUMA VASE, decorated with boldly-formed dragon in raised work. Height 7 inches.

382 Handsome carved jade-stone Bowl, fine white color. Height and diameter 2x4 inches.

383 MAGNIFICENT SOLID SILVER DAIMIO BOX, most skillfully wrought and inlaid with precious metals, gold lined.
   One of the finest specimens of metal-work ever brought to this country.

384 Small ivory Vase, gold lacquer ornamentation of bird, pine tree, etc.

385 Superb black and gold lacquer sectional Confection Box, 3 compartments, each compartment beautifully ornamented with pure gold. 4x5 inches.

386 EXTRAORDINARY SPECIMEN OF RAISED WORK, Satsuma Saki Bottle, ornamented with marvelously modeled carp fish, turtle, crab, frog, and lobster. Height 7 inches.

387 Valuable "moss green" carved jade-stone Bowl, highly polished, extremely rare in color.

388 Elegant lacquered Vase, cylindrical form, artistically ornamented with Japanese figure, flying storks, etc.   Height 6 inches.

389 SET BEAUTIFUL HAMMERED SILVER AFTER DINNER COFFEE CUPS AND SAUCERS, made in form of lotus leaves, all washed with gold.   Exhibition service, and only set known to be in existence.

390 Splendid wrought-iron Vase, beautifully inlaid with gold, silver-lined.   Height 10 inches.

391 Handsome black and gold lacquer Sweetmeat Box.

392 Fine Ohta ware Bowl, handsomely decorated with lotus plant, "Zogan" work, etc.

393 REMARKABLY FINE SPECIMEN OF IVORY CARVING, Magnificent Vase with cover supported by figures of dolphins, dragon handles, dog Foo surmounting cover.   Height and diameter 12x18 inches.   Finest specimen of Chinese carving ever offered at public sale.

394 Beautiful leaf shape Tray, exquisitely decorated by the great artist Tai-Zan.

395 WONDERFUL SATSUMA BOWL, SHOWING MARVELOUS ORNAMENTATION AND DECORATION IN RELIEF WORK AND PAINTING, SPECIAL ATTENTION BEING PAID TO EVERY DETAIL.   Height and diameter $3x4\frac{1}{2}$ inches.

396 —— ANOTHER BOWL equally as fine, same ware, but different style of ornamentation, being decorated with figures, landscape scene, etc., in rich enamels and gold embossed work.   Height and diameter 3x4 inches.
The above specimens together with two others recently sold in the Raymond collection at New York, were procured at the late Japanese Exhibition held at Nagasaki, when they were exhibited as, and acknowledged by experts to be wonderful examples of pottery and decorative art.

397 VALUABLE SPECIMEN AND GREAT CURIOSITY. Toucan Bird's head with beautiful plumage and artistic carving on bill.

398 MARVELOUSLY WROUGHT BRONZE PLAQUE, scene from Japanese mythology, figure of god and rain dragon in bas-relief, example of the famous artist in bronze, Foo-Wun, who ranks next to the great Saymin.   Height 10x12 inches.

399 MATCHLESS SPECIMEN OF CLOISONNE ART, MAG-
NIFICENT JAR WITH COVER. BLUE MEDALLIONS
WITH DESIGNS OF FLYING STORKS, QUAILS,
PHEASANTS, DUCKS, FLOWERS, ETC. SUPERB
COMBINATION OF COLORS ON BLACK GROUND,
BORDERS, BALL SURMOUNTING COVER, THE
WORK ON WHICH EXCELS (WITH BUT ONE
EXCEPTION), ANY SPECIMEN OF JAPANESE CLOI-
SONNE ENAMEL EVER SHOWN IN THIS COUNTRY.
Height and diameter 12x9 inches.

400 ELEGANT PLAQUE equally as fine, by same artist, has
gold and silver wires. Diameter 14 inches.

401 MAGNIFICENT NAGASAKI DINNER SERVICE made to
order and guaranteed to be the only set in this country,
decoration of a rich and artistic character in crimson and
gold, comprises large soup tureen and stands, 4 oval
covered vegetable dishes, fish dish, 3 meat dishes, 2 sauce
tureens and stands, 2 water pitchers, 2 bread trays, 2 relish
plates, 2 shell-shape pickle trays, 36 dinner plates, 18 soup
plates, 18 dessert plates. 101 pieces

402 Handsomely wrought Gorosa bronze Hibachi, dragons, birds,
etc., in bas-relief in panels, exceedingly fine in color and
workmanship. Height and diameter 9x12 inches.

403 Valuable antique Iron Vase, gold zogan work, made by the
celebrated metal-worker Koitz. Height 8 inches.

404 Exquisitely decorated Kiyoto goblet shape Vase, flying storks,
flowers, etc. Height 8 inches.

405 Pair superbly decorated Nagasaki Vases. Height 9 inches, extremely fine, Exhibition specimen.

406 Seto porcelain flower Pail, choice blue decoration.

407 SKILLFULLY WROUGHT BRONZE BOX AND COVER,
remarkable representation of basket work, vine and snail in
relief on cover, 6x10x7 inches, example of Gorosa.

408 ELEGANT CLOISONNE ENAMEL BRONZE FINGER Bowls, choice
colors and design. 12 pieces

409 Handsome Japanese Fabric Case, containing one dozen
cloisonné enamel individual salt stands, sold as 13 pieces

410 Rare Chinese "splash" Vase, biberon form, with five necks,
rich *rosedon* glaze, with shadings of purple. Height and
diameter 15x9 inches.

411 PAIR HIGHLY VALUABLE OLD SATSUMA VASES,
marvelously decorated with bold figure of Buddhist gods,
children, imps, etc., enameled dragons at necks. Heigh
20 inches. Extraordinary specimen. 2 pieces

412 REMARKABLY FINE BRONZE PIECE, CANDLESTICK
formed of lotus stem, leaf forming base, figure of imp,
frog and snail in relief. Height 13 inches. A carefully
modeled piece, and rare specimen.

413 Handsomely decorated Hezin porcelain Bowl.

414 Fine blue decorated Owari porcelain Tile, nickel-plated, and wood mountings.

415 MAMMOTH CLOISONNÉ ENAMEL PLAQUE, HIGHEST GRADE OF JAPANESE INLAID ART ON BRONZE, BEAUTIFUL DESIGN OF FLYING EAGLE, BIRDS, WATER SCENE, BAMBOO TREES, LOTUS FLOWERS, ETC., ON FINE BLUE COLOR GROUND, EXQUISITE BLACK GROUND BORDER. DIAMETER 32 INCHES. Please examine carefully.

416 MARVELOUSLY WROUGHT BRONZE GROUP, THREE FINELY MODELED FIGURES, REPRESENTING JAPANESE LADY OF COURT, AND ATTENDING PAGES, ALL MOUNTED ON A WONDERFULLY WROUGHT BRONZE STAND. 12x21x10 INCHES.

The above is without doubt a truly wonderful specimen of bronze work, exhibited as a master-piece of the artist at the late Nagasaki Exhibition.

417 BEAUTIFUL ANTIQUE IMARI KORA, unusually fine decoration and form, lotus flowers in relief, on sides. Height and diameter 15x21 inches. An exceedingly fine specimen of decorative and pottery art.

418 PAIR MAGNIFICENT SILVER BRONZE VASES, beautifully wrought and inlaid with gold and silver, made to order. Workmanship of the highest class. Height 17 inches.

2 pieces

Rich Embroideries.

419 MAGNIFICENT HANGING, black satin richly embroidered with brilliant colors of silk and gold bullion, lined with gold embossed cloth. 6x12 feet.

420 Elegant blue satin Table Cover, profuse embroidery in black silk of crows, 52x52 inches.

421 Splendid black satin Cover, beautifully embroidered, floral border, silver braid border, 54x54 inches.

422 Elegant crape Table Cover, richly embroidered and painted with figures of Japanese children at play, white or sacred elephant, flowers, etc., silk fringe border, gold embossed cloth lining, 52x52 inches.

423 Beautiful crape Hanging or Screen Center, artistically painted decoration of willow tree, branches, and birds, 27x36 inches.

424 —— Another, handsomely embroidered and painted, tree in blossom, bird, etc., 27x36 inches.

425 Square Embroidery, fan medallions, flowers, etc., 26x28 inches, crape lining.

426 Japanese paper Table Covers, illuminated border.

427 —— Another.

428 —— Another.

429 ELABORATELY EMBROIDERED PALACE HANGING, worked in gold bullion and silk, wonderful specimen of needle work, 55x78 inches.

ELEGANT LACQUERED AND TEAKWOOD FURNITURE, SCREENS, ETC.

430 ELABORATELY CARVED CHINESE TEAKWOOD CABINET, irregular form, made to order for Messrs. Vantine & Co.

431 Chinese teakwood Armchair, European shape, finely carved, upholstered in the white.   2 pieces

432 Handsomely carved teakwood pedestal Table, two-shelf, India marble top.

433 —— Another.

434 SUIT ELEGANT JAPANESE LACQUERED CHAM-BER FURNITURE, comprising bedstead, dressing-case, dressing bureau, chest of drawers, and small table. The above made to order, and believed to be the only suit in this country.

435 Handsomely lacquered daimio Screen, inlaid with ancient sword hilts, fine specimen of metal work.

436 Daimio Chair from the tycoon's palace at Yeddo.

437 Set handsomely decorated Chinese teapoy Table, black and gold.   4 pieces

438 —— Another set, different style.   4 pieces

439 —— Another set.   4 pieces

440 Handsome folding Screen, high form, 6 folds, fine embroidered silk panels.

441 Finely painted Screen, 4 folds, high form, white ground.

442 Richly lacquered Screen, 2 folds.

443 Chinese Bird Cage, house shape.

444 —— Another, medium.

445 —— Another, small.

446 MAGNIFICENT SATSUMA INCENSE BURNER, globular form on tripod support, decoration of a highly artistic order, bold figure of dogs Foo for handles and surmounting cover, rich gold embossed work. Height and diameter 19x17 inches.

447 PAIR BEAUTIFULLY DECORATED ANTIQUE IMARI VASES, interesting form, and highly decorative. Height 22 inches.   2 pieces

Friday Evening Sale.

448 Fruit shape Ink Wells, modern Corean ware.   2 pieces

449 Curious hanging Vase, bamboo form.

450 Fine cloisonné enamel Cups.   2 pieces

451 Awata ware small Teapots, neatly decorated.   2 pieces

452 Exquisitely decorated Kaga Vase, bamboo feet.

453 Beautifully decorated Hezin porcelain Bowl.

454 Very fine "splash" Vase, choice color of glaze. Height 6 inches.

455 Pair handsome cloisonne enamel Vases.   2 pieces

456 Rich blue decorated Owari porcelain Fruit Stand.

457 Porcelain Tile or Teapot Stand, choice blue decoration beneath glaze.

458 Curious earthen-ware Vase, representation of stump of tree, locusts, in white porcelain in relief.

459 Fine Nankin Bowl, finely decorated.

460 Ohta-ware figure Japanese priest.

461 Rare "Zogan" Vase, silver network on black ground.

462 Carved jade-stone Vase.

463 Beautifully decorated Hezin porcelain Plaque. Diameter 14 inches.

464 Valuable Corean Bowl, figure of crayfish and crabs in relief, shell supports.

465 Japanese cloisonne enamel cylinder Vase, choice in design and color. Height 10 inches.

466 Seto porcelain Saki Jugs, decoration in blue.   2 pieces

467 Antique Imari Bowl, brilliantly decorated.

468 Rare carved Jadeite-stone Writing Case.

469 Handsome specimen of pottery, basket with fruit in relief. Example of Makudza.

470 Choice turquoise blue Vase, fine in color. Height 6 inches.

471 Pair neatly decorated Awata-ware Vases. Height 8 inches.
          2 pieces

472 Elegant Japanese cloisonne enamel large Plaque, design of bird and bamboo branches on blue ground, rich border. Diameter 18 inches.

473 —— Another, smaller, equally as fine, design of storks, bamboo trees, crysanthemum, etc.

474 Valuable old Satsuma Figure, one of the seven household gods, decoration in gold and colors finely executed. Height 8 inches.

475 Pair superb Nagasaki Vases, exquisite gold decoration of bamboo trees on gray glaze. Height 10 inches.　2 pieces

476 Handsome Owari porcelain large Bowl, rich blue decoration.

477 Antique Japanese bronze Incense Burner, figure of priest on sacred bull, extremely old, and finely wrought.

478 Handsome Awata ware after dinner Coffee Cups and Saucers.　12 pieces

479 Finest quality black and gold lacquer oblong Tray.

480 HIGHLY VALUABLE OLD SATSUMA KORA, raised work ornamentation of boldly modeled dragons, figure of dog Foo on cover. Height and diameter, 18x7½ inches, unusually fine specimen of raised work.

481 Pair exquisitely decorated Kiyoto porcelain Vases, fan-shape and floral medallions, gold clouding. Height 12 inches.　2 pieces

482 Handsome Pekin Fans, gold and silver ornamentation, feather tips.　2 pieces

483 —— Other different.　2 pieces

484 Japanese cloisonné enameled porcelain Tea Jars, handsome design in bright colors.　2 pieces

485 Handsomely decorated Arita porcelain Bowl.

486 Exquisitely decorated old Satsuma Teapot, quaint shape.

487 Rare and curious Corean Vase, very fine representation of basket work, lifelike figure of crabs and cray-fish in relief. Height 21 inches.

488 Pair handsome Chinese antique crackle ware Vases, mustard brown and white glaze, imitation bronze ornamentation. Height 24 inches.

489 Choice "bleu de Nankin" oblong Tray.　2 pieces

490 Rare Imakura Bowl, brown glaze, enameled and gold decoration.

491 Handsome Plate, finest porcelain, beautiful hawthorn blossom decoration.

492 BEAUTIFUL ANTIQUE IMARI VASE, gourd shape, vines and blossoms in bold relief. Height 14 inches.

493 Pair Chinese crackle ware Vases, brown glaze, decoration of historical scenes, etc., painted in brilliant colors. Height 18 inches.　2 pieces

494 Handsomely decorated Nankin porcelain Broth Bowl, Cover, and Plate.

495 Pair choice cloisonné enamel Flower Vases.　2 pieces

496 Splash Vase, biberon form, with five necks, liver red glaze. Rare.

497 Pair very fine Satsuma small Vases, painted decoration of fishes beneath network of gold raised work, crabs and crayfish on the outside.   Height 7 inches.   2 pieces

498 Exquisitely decora'ed Kiyoto porcelain Flower Pail, gold clouding.

499 Choice hawthorn Tea Jar, very fine piece of porcelain and color.

500 MAGNIFICENT SATSUMA VASE, beautiful form and most artistic decoration, gathering of gods, deities, etc,, Japanese festive scene, colors exquisitely blended with pure gold. Height 22 inches ; an unsurpassed specimen of decorative art.

501 PAIR ELABORATELY CARVED GOROSA BRONZE VASES, birds, dragons, storks, mythological beasts, etc., in high relief, figures of rats for handles, serpent and hawk surmounting covers, made in sections and have movable bases. Height 30 inches ; extraordinary specimen of modern bronze work.   2 pieces

502 Elegant Arita porcelain hexagonal Plaque, exceedingly fine decoration, b ue glaze center.   Diameter 18 inches.

503 Brilliantly decorated Hezin porcelain Bowl, low flat form.

504 Exquisitely decorated Kaga Teapot.

505 Beautifully decorated Nagasaki Sweetmeat Jar, enameled blossoms, vines, etc., in rich colors.   5x9 inches.

506 Beautiful Kiyoto porce'ain Jar and Cover, exquisitely painted and enameled decoration of flying storks, lotus plants, etc., two co'ors of glaze, butterfly handle to cover.   Height and diameter 12x7 inches.

507 Pair richly lacquered Arita porcelain Vases, pure gold ornamentation of storks, pheasant, pine tree, etc., crimson and b'ack panels.   Height 17 inches.   2 pieces

508 Rare celadon Plate, decorated with figures of daimio lady and priest.

509 Very fine "bleu de Nankin" Vase, center vase with five smaller ones surrounding, all made in one piece.   Rare and fine.

510 Choice specimen of "Zogan" work, small Saucer, gold on dull chocolate ground.

511 Handsomely wrought Gorosa bronze Piece, figure of Japanese Bacchus standing on edge of Saki bowl, supporting vase or incense burner, base in representation of rocks and water, exceedingly fine in workmanship and color.   Used on certain ceremonial occasions.   Height 11 inches.

512 PAIR VERY ELEGANT OLD SATSUMA VASES, jar-shape, artistically painted, and exquisite gold embossed decoration of Japanese figures, vase of flowers, etc., in medallion, elephant head handles. Height 20 inches. Remarkably fine specimens of genuine old satsuma. 2 pieces

513 Fine Imari porcelain Bowl, dragon decoration in crimson and gold, green borders. Diameter 9 inches.

514 Set elegant Nagasaki porcelain after-dinner Coffee Cups and Saucers, exquisite decoration of bamboo branches in crimson and gold. 12 pieces

515 Finest black and gold lacquer oblong Tray, gold ornamentation.

516 Finely wrought antique bronze Candlestick, dragon in relief, example of Gorosa. Height 12 inches.

517 Handsome Kiyoto porcelain Vase, straight form, bamboo pattern, remarkably fine painting, tigers in snow storm, signed by artist. Height 13 inches.

518 Splendid Hiogo Vase, interesting form, "splash" glaze, finely painted, decoration of birds, fruits, blossoms, etc. Height 12 inches.

The above two vases are from the Nagasaki Exposition.

519 Richly decorated Nankin porcelain Punch Bowl, has carved teak-wood stand.

520 Superb old Satsuma small Vase, beautiful embossed decoration of flower-text, etc. Height 7 inches.

521 Fine Kiyoto porcelain cup-shape Vase, "zogan" decoration in gold and silver.

522 Choice cloisonné enamel Toilet Box, design of locust, butterfly, and detached flowers on red ground.

523 Fine antique Kiyoto Bowl, decorated with boldly drawn head of Buddhist priest.

524 Handsome Makudza Vase, remarkably fine representation of basket-work, gray glaze. Height 10 inches.

525 Pair elegant silver bronze Vases, exquisitely inlaid with gold, silver, and Gorosa bronze. Height 12 inches. 2 pieces

526 Set finely decorated Arita porcelain Bowls. 2 pieces

527 Handsome Tête-à-tête Set, finest Kiyoto porcelain, exquisitely decorated fan-shape medallions, etc. Sold with carved wood Tray.

528 Handsome lacquered Dressing-case, inlaid with pearl.

529 Rare Nankin Bowl, rich olive glaze, *metallic luster*.

530 Nankin porcelain sweet-meat Stands, enameled floral decoration. 2 pieces

531 Small Plates, decorated to match. 12 pieces

532 ELEGANT HEZIN PORCELAIN UMBRELLA STAND, beautifully decorated with cherry tree in blossom, bamboo branches, etc., on lavender color glaze, illuminated bands, crests in relief. Height and diameter 24x10 inches.

533 PAIR VALUABLE ANTIQUE CLOISONNE ENAMEL VASES, birds, flowers, etc., in green ground medallions, mosaic borders. Height 24 inches. Unusually fine in color and well preserved. 2 pieces

534 Pair fine porcelain Stands, enameled decoration. 2 pieces

535 Splendid Nagasaki Plaque, rich lacquered ornamentation, 15x17 inches.

536 Very fine *rosadon* Vase, bottle shape. Height 8 inches. Chinese "Splash."

537 Rare Imakura Vase, trumpet shape, peculiar splash glaze, top and bottom, bowl decorated in b'ue. Height 9 inches.

538 Fine Nankin Card Plate, richest Chinese decoration, gold ground border, teak-wood stand.

539 Celadon Punch Bowl, finest Chinese porcelain.

540 EXCEEDINGLY FINE SPECIMEN OF CLOISONNE ART, elegant jar shape Vase, exquisite design of peacock, pheasant, pine tree, etc., beautiful combination of colors, many of the cloisons filled with translucent enamels. Height 10 inches. Rare and valuable specimen.

541 Pair handsome Kiyoto Vases, finest porcelain and decoration, locust handles. Height 12 inches. 2 pieces

542 Kaga Plaque, bright color decoration.

543 Set Pekin enameled Confection Trays, forms table center piece. 7 pieces

544 ELEGANT CABINET, inlaid with various woods, has 6 drawers and enclosure, 12x24x12 inches.

545 Rich turquoise blue Vase, choice in color. Height 12 inches.

546 PAIR UNUSUAL CHINESE CRACKLE WARE VASES, white glaze, dragon, tiger, and stork in relief, decorated in b'ue. Height 24 inches. 2 pieces

547 Valuable Chinese celadon Temple Incense Jar, engraved decoration beneath glaze. Height and diameter, 25x16 inches.

548 PAIR MAGNIFICENT KAGA LARGE VASES, hexagonal form, with movable stands richly decorated with birds, flowers, etc., in panels, crimson and gold borders, vines and flowers in relief, forming handles. Height 22 inches. 2 pieces

549 VALUABLE OLD SATSUMA TEMPLE INCENSE JAR, BEAUTIFUL FORM, DECORATION EXECUTED IN A MASTERLY MANNER. SCENES FROM JAPANESE MYTHOLOGY IN MEDALLIONS AND IN BORDER AT BASE OF JAR, FINE COLORS ON ALTERNATE STRIPES SURROUNDING MEDALLIONS. HEIGHT AND DIAMETER 32x18 INCHES.

550 Pair very large Vases, finest Hezin porcelain, richly lacquered ornamentation in gold, crimson and black panels.
Height 38 inches.   2 pieces

551 MAGNIFICENT SCREEN, handsomely carved teak-wood
frame and mountings, richly embroidered black satin center,
protected by glass.

Valuable Kake-Monos,

MOSTLY ANCIENT EXAMPLES, FINELY PAINTED ON SILK, AND RICHLY MOUNTED.

552 Kake-Mono, crysanthemum flowers and flying bird.

553 —— Another, figure of Daimio.

554 —— Another, domestic scene.

555 —— Another, birds and flowers, brilliant colors.

556 —— Another, very fine India ink drawing, gathering of poets,
mountain scenery, etc.

557 —— Another, Japanese rice merchant.

558 —— Another, flowers and insects, bright colors.

559 —— Another, historical subject. ,

560 —— Another, street scene in Yokohama.

561 —— Another, Sketch in India ink, mythological subject.

562 —— Another, Da mio lady, plum tree in blossom, etc.

563 —— Another, Japanese mythological subject.

564 —— Another, landscape view, figures, etc.

565 —— Another, large scene on Lake Beaver, very finely painted.

566 —— Another, very large and exceeding'y fine, scenes from
Japanese mytho ogy, painted by famous Chinese artist.

567 REMARKABLE SCROLL. Subject, Japanese Idea of Hell.

THE JAPANESE IDEA OF HELL.

One of the most curious Hangings ever exhibited. It portrays the
infernal regions according to the Japanese idea. The first scene
represents Satan on earth seeking new victims. The arch fiend as
a sulphuric yellowish demon with protruding horns, cloven feet, and
a demoniacal expression luring his victims into his net, and plung-
ing them into fiery depths. They appear to fall into a nest of
burning scorpions, where they are tantalized by a glimpse of their
friends enjoying themselves in a lake of cool water. In the next
scene Satan takes the form of an immense dragon, with his human
victims crouching in terror at his feet. They are mercilessly dragged
into court, and the judge is represented as condemning them to be

tied to the rocks, and to have red hot lead poured down their throats. They are then chased by hyenas through a field of open knives and other sharp instruments. The victims are next portrayed as being tortured by having their limbs sawn off, and being thrown into a revolving wheel of fire. Satan next appears to be looking out for new victims on a field of battle. Some of these victims are made to hug red-hot stove-pipes, while Satan himself is fanning them. Others are swimming in seas of blood, surrounded by laughing demons. Others, still, are seated in a cauldron of red-hot sulphur, having their tongues pulled out. Some are represented as carrying heavy burdens of coal and throwing it into the fire to burn new victims. His Satanic majesty is next represented as feeding his subjects with rice, presumably to give them strength with which to endure greater tortures.

568 ELABORATELY EMBROIDERED PALACE HANGING, worked in silk and gold bullion, wonderful specimen of needlework, 58x74 inches.

569 Chinese Bird Cage.

570 —— Another, medium.

571 —— Another, small.

572 Cocoanut fiber brooms.   6 pieces